There's a Pot on my Belly

Trixie, the Pot-Belly pig, teaches a new
way of looking at beauty and brains.

as told to

Margo Mayberry

Illustrated by Phyllis Stewart

Copyright

Copyright 2010 by Margo Mayberry
There's a Pot on my Belly ISBN 1456323016   9781456323011
www.createspace.com

Cover Design, illustrations and layout by Phyllis Stewart
Phyllis can be contacted at pstewart0831@sbcglobal.net
Thanks to Dreamstime and ScrappersGuide for design elements.

Margo can be contacted at wheresduffybook@wowway.com

All profits from this book will go to help support the
Second Chance Pet Adoption Agency.
Their staff of volunteers has helped thousands of dogs and cats find happiness in this world despite the hardships that took them into the care of the shelter. Their dedication to finding forever homes for their charges is greatly appreciated.

Printed in the USA

Dedication

This book is dedicated to those volunteers who rescue all breeds of dogs from puppy mills and help them find their forever happy homes.

It is dedicated to all the animals still trapped in puppy mills until the rescue groups can get to you. It is also dedicated to the humans who work so hard to help animals find forever homes where they can live their lives in peace, safety, and happiness.

It is also dedicated to those kind, loving people who rescue cats, horses, goats, pigs and other animals from unsafe and unhealthy places and give them happy forever homes.

`There's a pot on my belly...

Well, there may not truly be a pot on my belly, but it sure looks like it sometimes if you look at me at just the right angle. My name is Trixie and I am a Pot-Belly pig, or so I am told by the humans who take care of me. I prefer to refer to myself as just "The Pig" of my farm. I live in Grove City, Ohio on a great little farm with many friends.

I am here to tell my story and dispel the myth that pigs are ugly and stupid and dirty. No way do I fit into any of those categories and my stories will definitely show you why.

My life began in a rather simple way. I was born into a litter of piglets to my dear mom on a small farm. My future human mom, Beth, heard about me and adopted both me and my two sisters to live on her farm.

Beth thought everyone needed a like-minded companion. That is why she has three horses, two goats, two miniature donkeys, three cats, and three dogs. She also thought she should have more than one pig.

Sadly, my sisters and I would fight all the time. We were just fighting for Beth's attention but it really stressed her out. We would bite each other's ears, push each other around, and genuinely be very, very grouchy to everyone else around us.

With all this fighting and squealing, our sibling rivalry proved to be too much for Beth, and my two sisters were sent to live with different neighbors close to the farm where I was born. Now, without each other's company, all three of us are happy and healthy.

At first I had no trouble defining myself as a pig. But soon, with the family that I now live with, I began to wonder... am I a pig? ... am I a dog? ... am I a cat or goat or donkey or even a horse? It was getting hard for me to tell in this big family who adopted me.

You see, they treated me the same way they treated all the other animals who lived on the farm. I had an outdoor pen of my own and a small dog house (or was it a pig house?) with a soft comfy cushion inside. I got to play and run in the yard, barns and fields with the other dogs and animals in the family. I also was allowed to relax inside Beth's farmhouse like they did, just the dogs and cats that is. (The donkeys, goats and horses were not welcome in the house.) I could jump on and off the furniture, snuggle on the couch with Beth, and even play ball in the house – a story of its own I will tell you about later.

My cat sister and brothers are named Riley, Sophie and Caesar. Riley is just a small grey and white cat and is very friendly to me. When I first got my outdoor pen set up, he would jump over the fence to say hello. *"This is a really nice cage,"* he would say. *"Can I hang out with you? Can I sleep in your pen with you?"* he would ask over and over again. Needless to say, we get along just great.

Sophie, the calico cat chooses to ignore me completely. It's as if I'm not even there, as far as she is concerned. Caesar, wearing his tuxedo, spends a lot of time outdoors in the barn, so we don't see him very often in the house.

With all us creatures around, Beth has many chances to take pictures!

My donkey sisters, Digger and Dusty, get a little nervous when I get into their pen to play though. They are notorious for chasing the cats and they seem to think I am some kind of a cat so they tend to chase me a lot if I get in their pen. They are not trying to hurt me, but have I mentioned that I can run really fast? That helps a lot.

Morty and Spicy, my goat sisters, chase me sometimes, too, but they seem like they are moving in slow motion compared to my dazzling speed.

Fatboy, my big white horse brother did not seem to mind my presence at all until one day I started to eat the grain that was dropping on the ground from his feeding trough. Boy, that got his attention fast! *"I'm going to bite you if you don't stop that,"* he said in a very loud voice that startled me. Horse feed is no longer on my favorite menu list of things to eat. Got to keep peace in the family, you know.

Running is regular exercise for me because there is one dog at the farm, a really big Rottweiler named Brutus, who always seems to want to chase me. He is basically a friendly dog, but he keeps running after me panting, *"Bacon, bacon, I smell bacon!"*

I have no idea why he keeps saying that but so far he has not caught me to explain what that means. I think I am happy about that fact. I also try not to make too much noise around him. He does not seem to understand my language very well either. He thinks I am some kind of squeaky plaything when I make my happy sounds and wants to toss me around like a toy.

Maddie is the most laid back and easy going of my dog sisters. She is a black Labrador mix and always wonders when she looks at me, *"Is that a dog – or what exactly is that?"*

She just lays around and watches me jumping up and down, chasing my ball, and glares at me as if to say, *"Don't mess with me, I am bigger than you."* If she is lying on the floor and I decide I want to jump down off the couch, she makes a great springboard to get from the couch to the floor, but she does NOT seem to appreciate that role in her life at all.

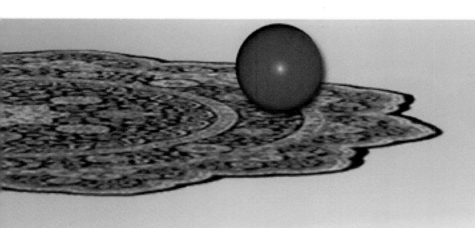

I like to meet new people also. When Beth's friends come to the farm, they come out to my pen and I get let out so I can run around in the yard and go into the house with them. I get really impatient, too. They stand there at the gate talking and I stand there saying, *"Grunt, snoot, grunt, oink, snoot, snoot, ggrrt, hemp. hrmpt, snpmt, squeek,"* over and over again. Sometimes they don't seem to understand that I'm saying, *"OK enough talking, let me out of here so I can run!"* And run I do. Have I mentioned that I can run really fast?

Snft grnt squeal, oink, squeek...

My main goal in life at this point is to eat food — and my definition of food is anything that catches my eye. My favorite thing to do is stand next to the refrigerator in the house waiting for that door to open. Inside that fridge is what humans call grapes. Green grapes, purple grapes, it doesn't matter which to me. I love them both.

I talk to Beth with whatever sounds I can make. I keep trying to tell her, *"I must eat, must eat. That looks like food, feed me. Is that for me? Food? More grapes please, please, please!"* All she seems to hear is, *"Snft grnt squeal, oink, squeek, hrmkph frmph grunt."*

hrmkph frmph grnt!

Beth says I am an omnivore. That means I can eat almost anything, and I do a really good job of that. I root in the grass and eat insects and grubs and ants. I run in the field and eat grass. Beth tells her friends if they need any grass removed to just call me. In rooting for the insects under the grass I can remove the sod real quick with my efficient nose.

Speaking of favorite foods, Beth has this interesting way of putting food in my dish. She puts rocks in the dish along with the food. That way I get to "root" out my food from underneath the rocks. Boy, is that fun. That fulfills my rooting instinct and keeps me busy longer so I don't get into as much mischief in the house (like trying to root under the carpet). There was one time when I was rooting in the pillows on the couch and got my nose stuck in the inside corner of the pillow case. I squeeked and squawked really loud until Beth heard me and came and rescued me from the pillow case.

We pigs like a very repeatable routine in our lives. For some reason, it is in our genes to like a schedule. So Beth installed this terrific automatic feeder in my pen. Around six o'clock every night I run like crazy to my pen because I KNOW that food will be automatically put into my dish and I need to get there to eat it before anyone else even knows it is there.

I must admit, my food is different from what the cats, horses, donkeys, goats and dogs around me eat. It seems like we each have our own special kind of food that is the best for us to eat to keep us healthy and happy.

Beth had to install this special feeder because I would keep knocking over the bulk container of food and just eat and eat. So this feeder is now out of my reach and at that special time of day it moves a lever and drops just the right amount of the food down where I can safely reach it. That does keep me from overeating and the running does help keep my figure slim and attractive. At first Beth had the auto feeder near the ground, but after I destroyed the second one, she put it up high where I can't reach it.

I know when it's mealtime, and have I mentioned that I can run really fast?

There are times, too, when I can get out of my pen by myself. I can run all over the farm while my dog sisters have to stay within their electric underground fence. They have special collars that stop them when they get to close to that fence. I have no collar so no fence can stop me, whether I can see it or not.

One day I made it all the way to the farm behind us. Beth was real sneaky though. She got me to come back by leaving a trail of grapes all the way back to my pen. She knows I can never say no to grapes. And to show you how smart I really am, by following that trail of grapes I knew I would get back to my pen just in time for my automatic feeder to drop more food for me to eat.

The only fence I have had a problem with was the fence around what Beth calls a hot tub. I was curious as to what that special tub was so I got my head between the slats of the fence around it and got stuck. Beth had to pull off some of the slats to get me out. I have not been near that fence since she repaired it!

One day Beth put this thing on me called a harness and took me for a walk on the walking path near the farm. For some reason I got the strangest comments from both people and dogs that we passed. "Is that a dog? What is that?" I heard people say.

"*Bacon, where is that bacon smell coming from?*" is the typical comment from the dogs I would pass.

Jojo, one of my other dog siblings says that, too sometimes. He lays on the couch and occasionally rises up to say, "*Hmmmm – bacon?*" I really have to find out what that statement means.

Sometimes running so fast gets me into trouble. Right inside the door of the house there is a section of the floor made of hardwood and if I get running too fast, which I always seem to do, I lose my balance totally. I end up skidding across the floor on either my back or my belly until I reach the carpeted area to get stopped. I can't seem to get any traction at all on that section of the floor. Beth seems to think that is funny and I can hear her laughing whenever I sail across the floor.

Things can get really bad when I am chasing my busy ball. This is one very special, to me anyway, type of playball. It gets filled with treats and when I roll the ball around with my nose, the treats drop out of the small holes in the ball. Boy, do I love that ball. I chase it all over the house and Beth can always tell where I am in the house by listening to what the ball is bumping into. One night when one of Beth's friends was visiting, she got to see first-hand how much I love that ball. I was just chasing it like I always do and this floor lamp got right in the middle of my path and fell over all by itself.

Crash! It ended up on the floor and Beth had to get all of us animals away from there so we would not step on the broken glass. I wonder what that expression she used means, "Bad piggy!" Hmmm.

I have no idea why that floor lamp jumped into the path of my ball. How dare it do that! Well, it will not do that anymore as that lamp is history.

Another day I was chasing my busyball when it ended up in the bathroom. Boy, was that a strange day. Every time the ball got near the bathtub, something hit the top of my head, "Fwap!" When I looked around I didn't see a thing. So I went back to pushing my ball and, "Fwap!" It happened again! I turned around really quickly and looked all around the room but didn't see what hit me. Quickly, I pushed the ball out of that room. I thought I heard Caesar, my black cat brother laughing in the background somewhere but I was leaving the room so fast I could not be sure.

I also want to explain my self created beauty treatment. People think pigs are so dirty but here is what I learned from watching that thing in the house called a television. I have seen women put these mud packs on their faces, and creams and ointments and when they take them off they call themselves so beautiful. So I had to try that.

I created my own beauty routine. When my water bowl gets filled, I push it over to the part of my pen where the grass has worn off, and then tip it over. Then I push the water all around in the dirt and make the greatest beauty mud pack ever invented. Next I rub it all over my face and as it starts to dry I rub it all off in the grass. Boy, does that make me look beautiful.

So you see – most people think of pigs as just wallowing in the dirt, but it is just a self-created beauty treatment. And it costs my owner nothing! A free mud pack facial, who can ask for anything more? And to think you thought pigs were just dirty. We just work hard making ourselves even more beautiful.

There is only one sad thing I have to report about in my home. Beth has this crazy pink thing she calls a tutu that she puts on me sometimes. I do NOT like that garment. I think I am getting that feeling across to Beth though because she doesn't put it on me except at a certain time of year humans call Halloween. Then all us animals get some kind of costume to commemorate the holiday. Boy, am I glad that only comes once a year!

I hope you can tell from my story that I am one very happy pig. I am beautiful thanks to my frequent mud pack facials. I am smart because I know where those grapes are stored. And I am sure Beth would not let me up on the couch if I was dirty.

So, there, all those myths about pigs being ugly, dumb and dirty are now dispelled and you now know the truth about how great a pet we pot-belly pigs can be.

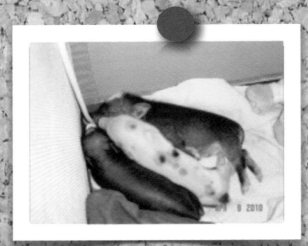

SAVE A LIFE.
SPAY OR NEUTER
YOUR PET.